MAGICAL
IDEAS

Written by
Helen Murray

Models by
Emily Corl,
Rod Gillies,
and **Kevin Hall**

CONTENTS

I HOPE YOU GET INSPIRED BY THESE MAGICAL LEGO BUILDS!

UNICORN FAMILY

Create a whole family of colorful unicorns with magical horns. Why not add wings to make extra-special unicorns that can fly?

SPECIAL BRICK

This horn piece makes a perfect unicorn horn—and comes in 13 colors! A cone or rod would also work well.

I WISH I COULD BE A UNICORN!

Slopes form tail

Stack two bricks for longer legs

DADDY UNICORN

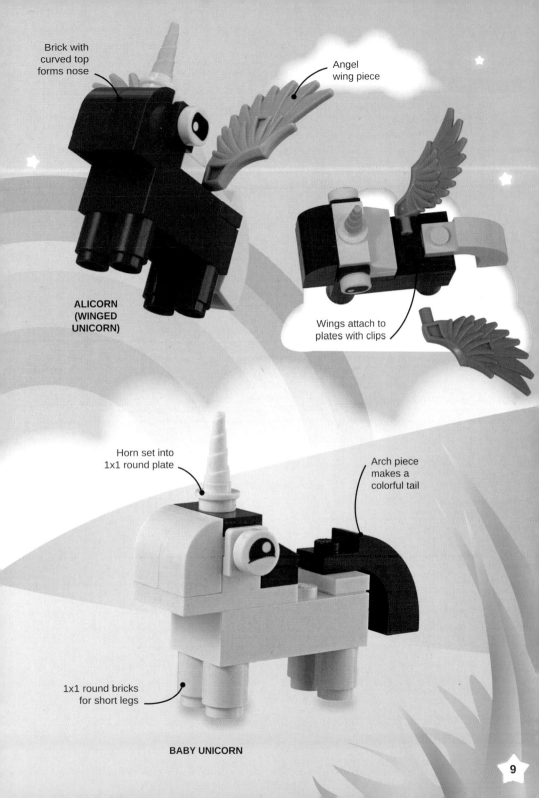

Brick with curved top forms nose

Angel wing piece

ALICORN (WINGED UNICORN)

Wings attach to plates with clips

Horn set into 1x1 round plate

Arch piece makes a colorful tail

1x1 round bricks for short legs

BABY UNICORN

ENCHANTED FOREST

What was that noise? A tree? It can't be!
Build a forest where all is not as it seems.
Give your trees peeking eyes and
open mouths.

THESE ARE
TREE-MENDOUS!

1x2 brick with
hole is perfect
for a chattering
mouth

Watchful
eyes

Toadstool

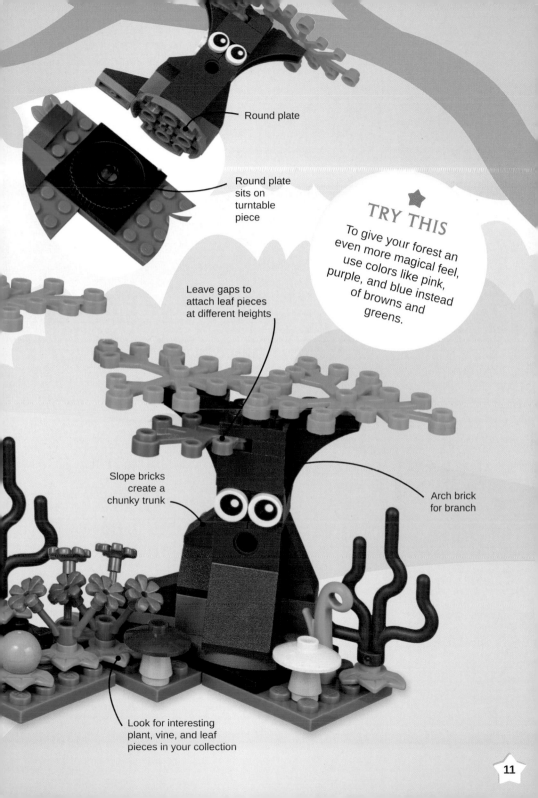

Round plate

Round plate sits on turntable piece

★
TRY THIS

To give your forest an even more magical feel, use colors like pink, purple, and blue instead of browns and greens.

Leave gaps to attach leaf pieces at different heights

Slope bricks create a chunky trunk

Arch brick for branch

Look for interesting plant, vine, and leaf pieces in your collection

FAIRY
FRIENDS

Do you believe in fairies? Make magical fairies with colorful wings and clothes. What adventures will your fairies get up to?

Add flowers to your fairy's hair

Minifigure head piece makes a stylish bun

HMPH! THIS FAIRY DUST GETS EVERYWHERE!

Slopes form skirt shape

Wings attach to angle plate on fairy's back

Arm connects to body with LEGO® Technic pin

2x2 plate secures angled plates

TRY THIS

Use different colored angled plates for multicolored wings. If you have wing pieces in your LEGO® collection, you could use those, too.

Fluttering eyes

Wings are four angled plates

Tiny fairy's wings are two small angled plates

Cone makes a perfect fairy skirt

Two pink plates make up the fairy skirt

FAIRY VILLAGE

Create beautiful homes for your fairy folk.
Build an inviting fairy garden with tiny houses,
or a cute cottage with a door for your little
LEGO fairies to live inside.

Brown leaf
piece

1x1 slope
brick as
a roof

Gray tiles for
a paved path

TRY THIS

Build a pond or a bridge
for your fairy garden. Why
not build furniture for your
fairy cottage, too? Make
a tiny table, chair,
or bed.

Toadstool

**FAIRY
VILLAGE**

Mini bird bath

HMM ... WHAT'S THE SPELL TO CLEAN MY ROOM?

LEGO Technic connector

LEGO Technic pin

This large flower makes the cottage look even smaller!

Chunky chimney

Keep your house hidden under some leaves

Round plate with hole for a window

Wand attaches to plate with clip

FAIRY COTTAGE

FAIRY

WELCOME FAIRIES

Invite magic into your home by building a door so that fairies can enter from a magical land. You could leave notes and tiny gifts for your fairy visitors, too!

The hole in the wall doesn't need to be exactly the same size as the door

Decorate with flowers—or anything else you like!

You could add fancy details like a rope cord doorbell

Tiles look like wooden slats

Door handle is plate with bar

Tiles attach to bricks with studs on the side

Door hinge is a bar that attaches to plates with clips

TOOTH FAIRY
BOX

Make the tooth fairy's job so much easier by creating a little box for your tooth to go inside. There might even be a surprise waiting for you in the morning!

Small space for tooth to sit inside

Slopes create jagged tooth shape

PUT YOUR TOOTH INSIDE!

Add eyes for extra cuteness

Wings are angled plates

Little legs look like ridges of a tooth

MYTHICAL CREATURES

There are many myths and legends about special animals who have a mix of fabulous features. Build a hippogriff, centaur, or faun—or why not make up your own fantastic beast?

Wing connects to plate with clip

Chest feather piece attaches to a brick with studs on the side

Eagle wings are angled plates

Plate with tooth makes perfect eagle's beak

1x1 angled plate and slope for horse hoof

HIPPOGRIFF (HALF HORSE, HALF EAGLE)

Long hair

Bushy horse tail

CENTAUR
(HALF HUMAN, HALF HORSE)

Human upper body

Curved bricks for horse legs

ONE MINUTE
I WANT CHOCOLATE.
THE NEXT, I WANT
GRASS!

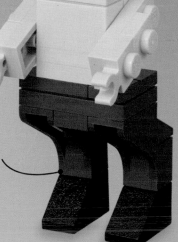

Slopes look like little goat horns

Neck is a jumper plate

★
SPECIAL BRICK

A 1x1 plate with clip is so handy. You can use it to attach something, but it also makes great features like hands, feet, and feathers.

Arch piece forms curved goat leg

FAUN (HALF HUMAN, HALF GOAT)

FLY AWAY

Go bird-watching—with a magical twist.
Build birds with flame or lightning pieces,
and you will have a phoenix that rises from the
flames or a bird that shoots lightning!

Add a
majestic
fiery crest

Wing is
wavy flame
piece

Grille piece for
chest feathers

Leg clips on to
a plate with bar

⭐ SPECIAL BRICK

The wavy flame pieces make
incredible phoenix wings.
You could also use it for
arms, blasters, or to
decorate a blazing
set of wheels!

PHOENIX

Transparent blue flame piece for crest

I'M SHOCKINGLY POWERFUL!

Lightning piece attaches to plate with clip

Chest feather is plate with tooth

LIGHTNING BIRD

Legs look like they are glowing!

WOAH! THAT IS SOME SPARROW!

If your bird has long, thin legs, pop it on a perch for extra stability.

WITCHING HOUR

Wait until it's dark outside and build a magical witch and her mischievous cat. Don't forget a pointy hat and broomstick!

Cone makes a perfect pointy hat

HEE, HEE, HEE!

Green bricks— for the classic witch look!

★
TRY THIS

What other animal helpers can you build with just a handful of bricks? How about a mouse or an owl?

Broomstick bricks attach above and below brick hand

Slopes form skirt shape

HUBBLE BUBBLE ... HERE COMES TROUBLE!

Just 12 pieces make up this cat!

Plate with tooth for the tail's tip

Yellow cone for brush

WISE WIZARD

Create an enchanted magic-maker with a beard and wand. What spells will your wizard cast?

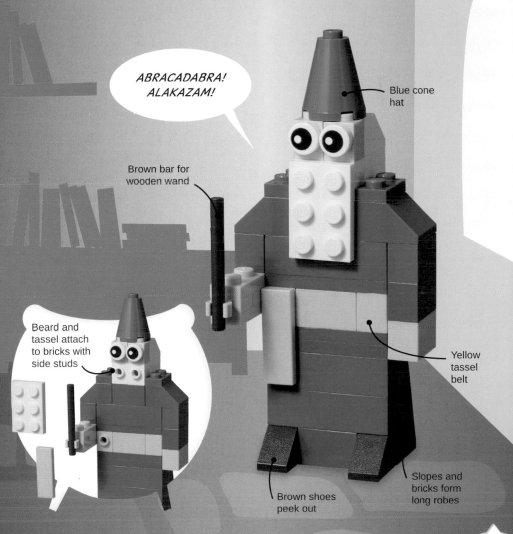

ABRACADABRA! ALAKAZAM!

Blue cone hat

Brown bar for wooden wand

Beard and tassel attach to bricks with side studs

Yellow tassel belt

Slopes and bricks form long robes

Brown shoes peek out

23

WAND
WORKSHOP

Cast a spell with a LEGO wand. Make a magician's wand, wizard's wand, or fairy wand—or see what other types of wands you can conjure up!

ALAKAZAM! I WAND-ER IF THAT WILL WORK?

Use curved slopes for a pointed shape

WIZARD'S WAND

Tan tiles and plates give an old-fashioned feel

Plate with vertical tooth

SPECIAL BRICK

This bar has a plate and stud built into it, which makes it perfect for a wand. You can add all kinds of fun decorations to it.

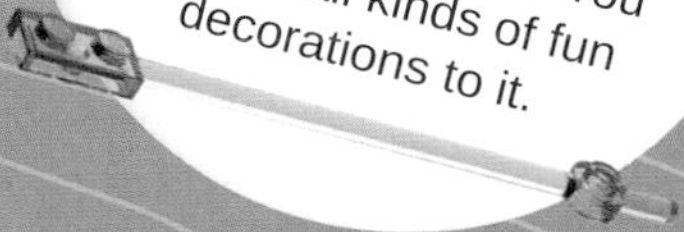

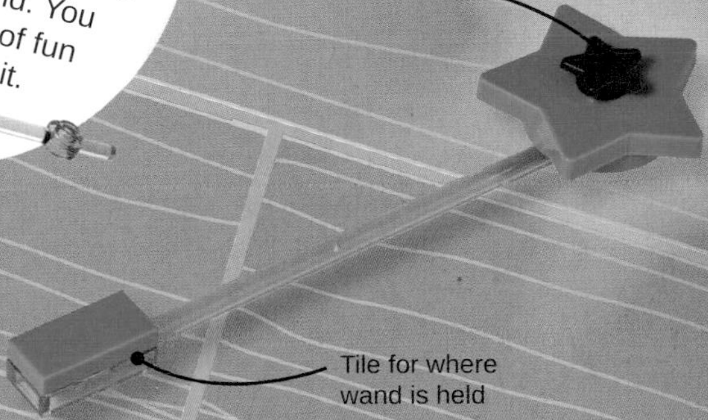
Star pieces make this wand look extra magical!
Tile for where wand is held
FAIRY WAND

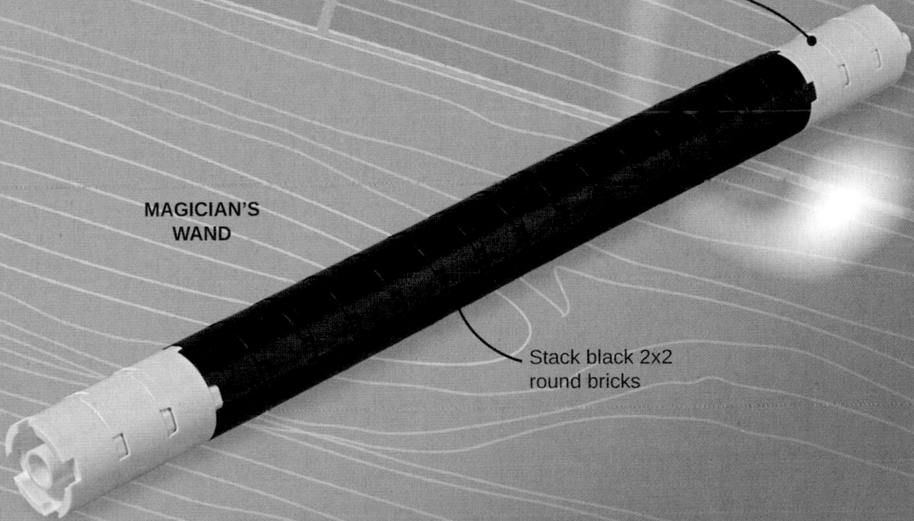
White 2x2 round bricks for tips
MAGICIAN'S WAND
Stack black 2x2 round bricks

POTIONS
CLASS

Fizz! Bubble! Bang! Build a potions workshop and stir a bewitching brew, mix powerful potions, and practice your spells.

Plate with clip to attach ingredients to the wall

Potion bottles

TAIL OF LIZARD, EYE OF NEWT ...

TOP TIP

Look for small transparent pieces in your collection. Tiny 1x1 round bricks and slopes are ideal for miniature potion bottles.

Bar piece for stirring

Hot coals

POTIONS WORKSHOP

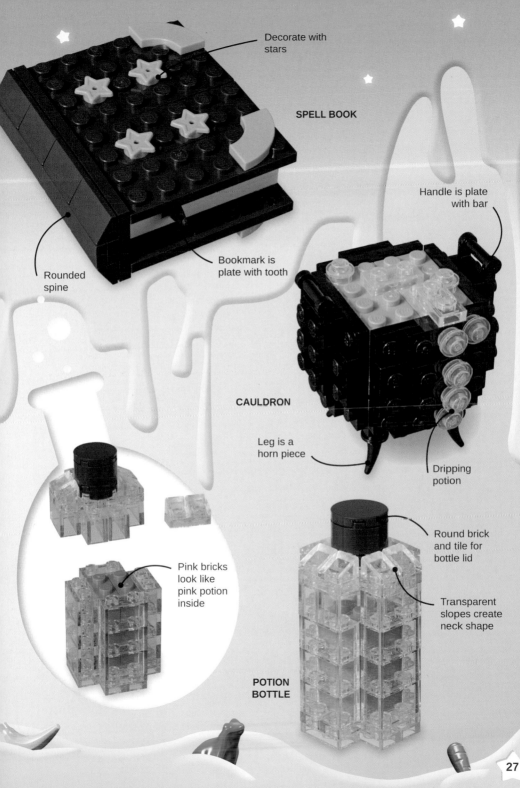

Decorate with stars

SPELL BOOK

Handle is plate with bar

Rounded spine

Bookmark is plate with tooth

CAULDRON

Leg is a horn piece

Dripping potion

Pink bricks look like pink potion inside

Round brick and tile for bottle lid

Transparent slopes create neck shape

POTION BOTTLE

AMAZING CHANGE!

Wow your friends with a spellbinding transformation. Just use a LEGO® turntable piece for a touch of magic!

Shield decoration

Push to rotate castle wall

AND NOW YOU WILL TURN INTO A FROG ...

Wall looks the same on both sides

MUCH BETTER!

Wall rotates on turntable piece built into the floor

Frog sits on seat that is identical to seat on other side

Prince is on the other side!

WEREWOLF CHUMS

Start building under the light of a full moon and you might just see your bricks transform into a pair of werewolf friends.

Pointy ear is 1x1 plate with horizontal tooth

ARRRROOOOO!

Human shorts from before the transformation

Fang is plate with vertical tooth

Slope bricks form legs and feet

SPECIAL BRICKS

A 1x1 plate with horizontal or vertical tooth can be used for all kinds of body parts.They make great teeth, ears, claws, beaks, and more.

Slope brick sits on top of slanted plates

1x2 plate with horizontal tooth for claws

UNDER THE
SEA

Create mermaids and mermen for magical adventures beneath the waves. Build a human top half and a dazzling tail for the bottom half.

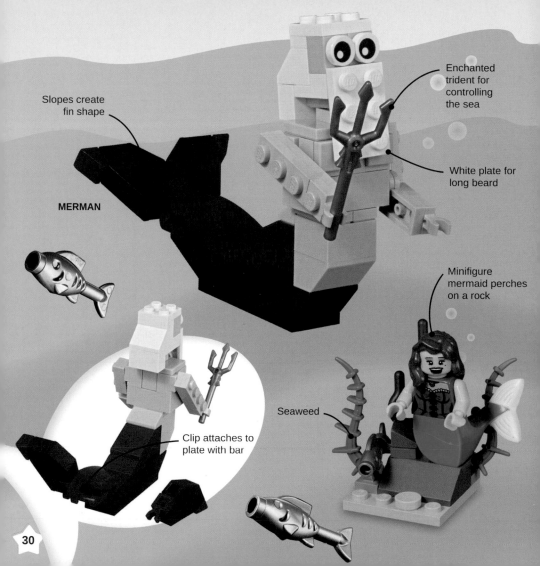

Slopes create fin shape

Enchanted trident for controlling the sea

White plate for long beard

MERMAN

Minifigure mermaid perches on a rock

Seaweed

Clip attaches to plate with bar

MERMAID

Long, flowing hair

Separate tail pokes out of the water

Pink mermaid top

I FEEL FIN-TASTIC TODAY!

Eye tile

⭐ **TRY THIS**

Build an underwater palace for your merpeople. Look for pieces that could work as treasure, shells, and plants to decorate it with.

1x1 slopes for fin tip

Plate with clip for hand

MERGIRL

SEA MONSTERS

Build a mysterious monster of the deep blue sea. Perhaps yours will have a long, eel-like body or lots of wriggly, squiggly arms!

★ SPECIAL BRICK

Curved arches are useful for adding rounded shapes to buildings, vehicles, and animals. They make especially good humps!

HELLOOOOO! OVER HERE!

Curved arches form rounded shape

Humps peek out of water

Striped neck

Blue plates for sea

SEA SERPENT

Short tentacle piece connects to brick with stud on side

Tentacle piece attaches to brick with hole

I NEVER SEE ANY UNUSUAL CREATURES ...

Long tentacle

Main body is made from just six small bricks!

Angled eyes for a funny expression

KRAKEN

GENIE IN A LAMP

Legend says that if you rub a magic lamp, a powerful genie will grant you three wishes. Why not try building your own? Remember: choose your wishes wisely!

★ TOP TIP

You don't need to have the exact same bricks to create a model. Use the idea as a starting point. Your genie will be magically unique!

YOUR WISH IS MY COMMAND...

Arms can be angled

Slopes form a smokelike lower body

Genie appears from the lamp's spout

Lamp handle

Curved slopes for rounded shape

UP, UP, AND AWAY

Get your head in the clouds—and imagine the world from way up high. A LEGO magic carpet can take your minifigures anywhere!

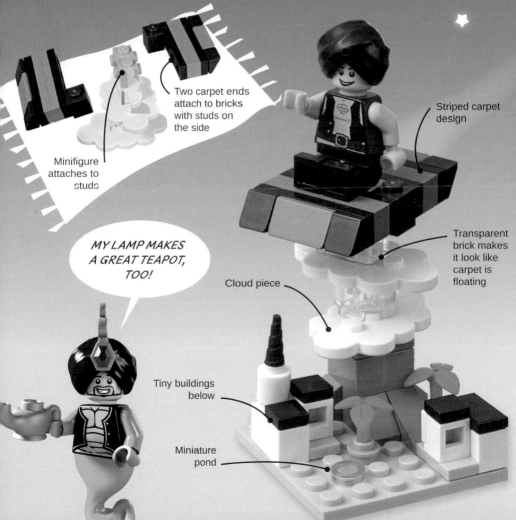

Two carpet ends attach to bricks with studs on the side

Minifigure attaches to studs

MY LAMP MAKES A GREAT TEAPOT, TOO!

Striped carpet design

Transparent brick makes it look like carpet is floating

Cloud piece

Tiny buildings below

Miniature pond

OPEN SESAME!

Build a hidden cave with mountains of gold and precious jewels. Who knows? There might just be something magical inside!

Arch-shaped brick for entrance

Cave is hidden under plants

Chest is bursting with treasure

Stacks of coins are 1x1 round plates and tiles

CAVE

Use different types of gray bricks for an uneven, crumbling cave wall

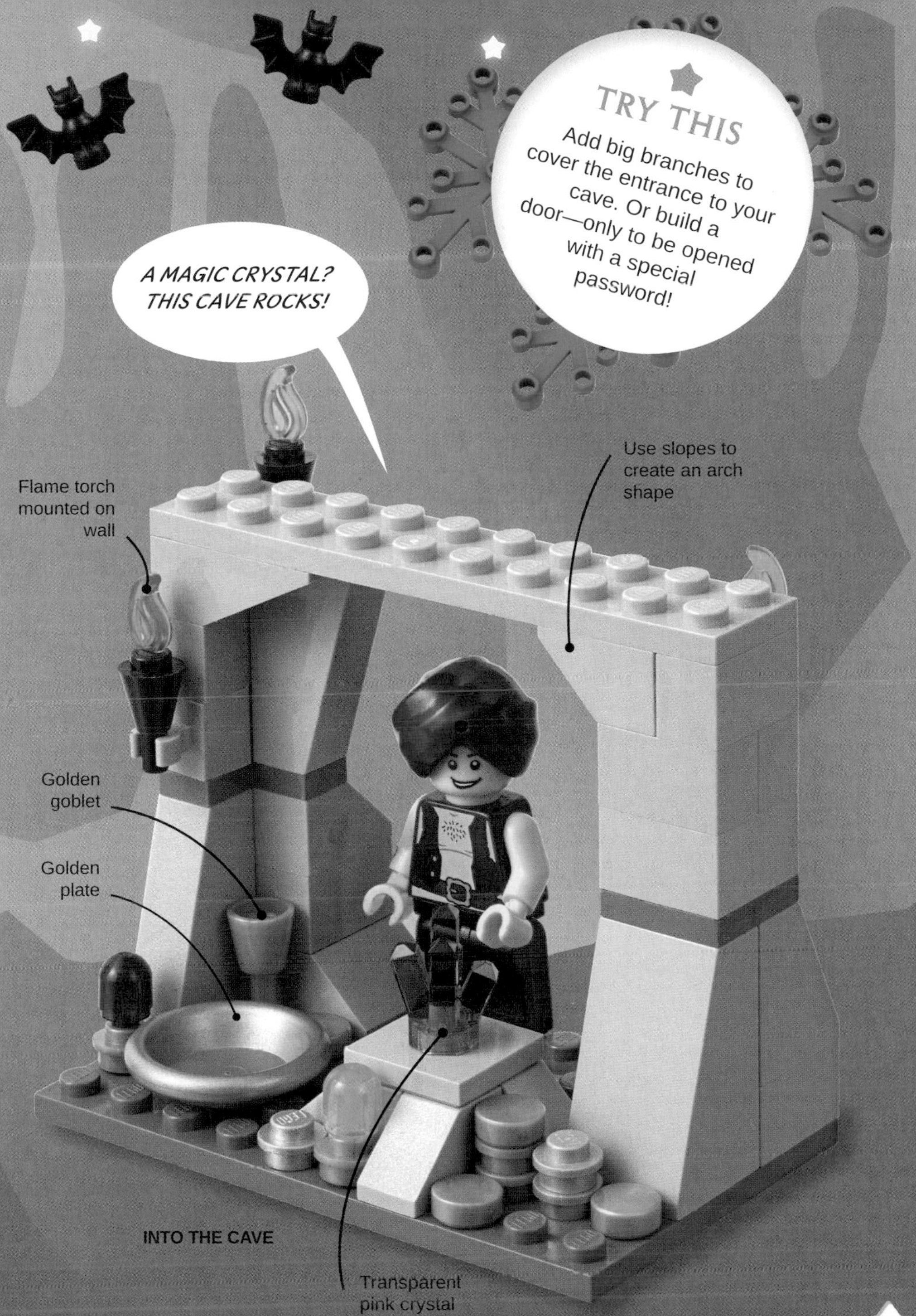
A MAGIC CRYSTAL? THIS CAVE ROCKS!
Flame torch mounted on wall
Use slopes to create an arch shape
Golden goblet
Golden plate
Transparent pink crystal

TRY THIS

Add big branches to cover the entrance to your cave. Or build a door—only to be opened with a special password!

INTO THE CAVE

LUCKY CHARMS

Feeling lucky? It doesn't matter if you're not!
Build yourself some good luck with a lucky
LEGO four-leaf clover, die, or horseshoe.

SPECIAL BRICK

This joyful heart plate also comes in red and dark pink. You'll feel lucky to have it in your collection!

Heart-shaped plate for leaf

Rare fourth leaf!

I HOPE I'M LUCKY ENOUGH TO FIND A POT OF GOLD!

One-stud-wide plates for stem

FOUR-LEAF CLOVER

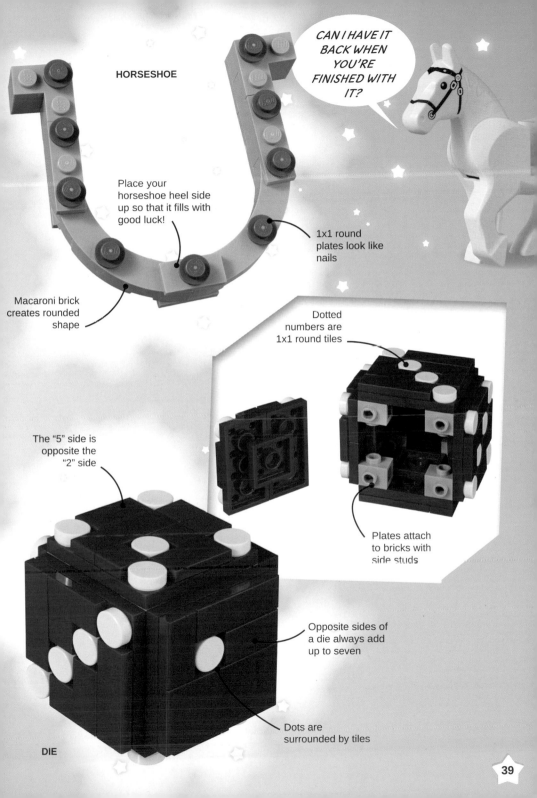

HORSESHOE

CAN I HAVE IT BACK WHEN YOU'RE FINISHED WITH IT?

Place your horseshoe heel side up so that it fills with good luck!

1x1 round plates look like nails

Macaroni brick creates rounded shape

Dotted numbers are 1x1 round tiles

The "5" side is opposite the "2" side

Plates attach to bricks with side studs

Opposite sides of a die always add up to seven

Dots are surrounded by tiles

DIE

ELF PARADE

Build a gang of elves for adventures in enchanted lands. This mini elf looks like she's on her way to the North Pole to help Santa Claus!

TOP TIP

Corner plates and hinge plates create a bent arm shape for LEGO figures.

Horn pieces make longbow

Slope for a pointy ear

Hinge plate

Layered plates for long hair

Corner plate

Long elven gown

ELF WARRIOR

Striped leggings

CHRISTMAS ELF

ELF ADVENTURER

TETCHY TROLLS

Trolls like to hide in caves or under bridges, so they can be hard to spot. Why not build your own? Be warned, though—trolls can be grumpy!

WHO'S THAT TRIP-TRAPPING OVER OUR BRIDGE?

TRY THIS

Trolls can be any size. See if you can build a troll from just a handful of bricks! Clips make perfect tiny hands.

Teeth are 1x1 round bricks

Downturned eyes look a little sad!

2x2 round brick creates a bulky arm

Belt detail

Angle plates for wide foot

41

SNOW QUEEN

A snow queen can freeze anything! She can create magnificent ice sculptures with an icy blast of her hand. Build a snow queen and her glistening ice creations.

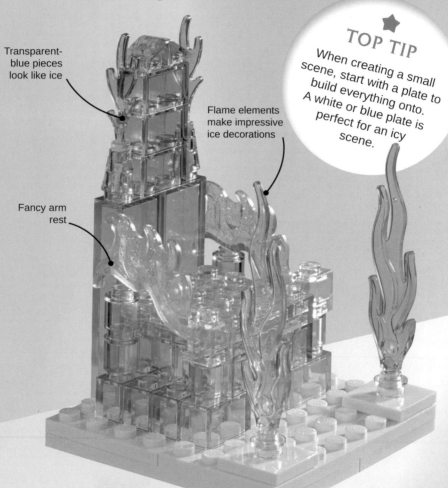

Transparent-blue pieces look like ice

Flame elements make impressive ice decorations

Fancy arm rest

★ TOP TIP

When creating a small scene, start with a plate to build everything onto. A white or blue plate is perfect for an icy scene.

ICE THRONE

NEXT, I'LL MAKE AN ICE-CREAM MACHINE!

MINI SNOW QUEEN

Sparkling ice crystal

Icicle

Ice palace wall

Hinge plate allows arm to bend

Long blue hair

Plate with handle on cape attaches to plate with clip

Transparent-blue flame piece for a magical icy blast

Cape is layered plates

White and blue layered gown

SNOW QUEEN

43

SILLY GIANT

Fee-fi-fo-fum ... I smell some teeny LEGO people below. Build a giant straight from a fairy tale. Decide whether you want yours to be fierce, friendly, or a bit silly!

1x1 round plates attach to bricks with studs on the side

THIS ICE CREAM IS DELICIOUS!

TOP TIP

Adding eyes gives character to your LEGO figures. If you don't have eye tiles, use 1x1 round plates, or try other small pieces.

Round tile for belt buckle

ISN'T THAT A HUGE CLUB?

Minifigure trophy looks like a tiny person below

Slope forms boot shape

MAGICAL GOOSE

Build a goose—and have fun imagining what you would do if you had a goose that could lay golden eggs!

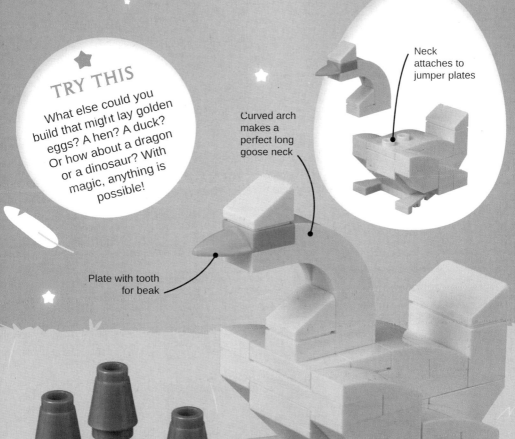

★ **TRY THIS**

What else could you build that might lay golden eggs? A hen? A duck? Or how about a dragon or a dinosaur? With magic, anything is possible!

Neck attaches to jumper plates

Curved arch makes a perfect long goose neck

Plate with tooth for beak

Eggs are gold 1x1 cones

Look for unusual yellow pieces for feet

45

FRIENDLY YETI

This yeti doesn't get to see many people because it lives up high in the remote mountains. Why don't you build another, so it can have a friend?

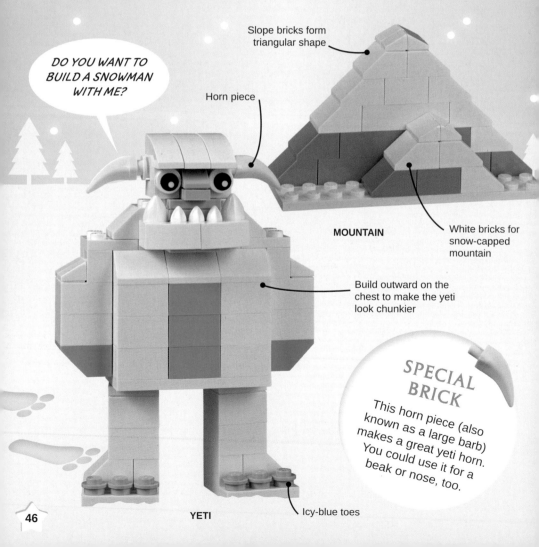

Slope bricks form triangular shape

DO YOU WANT TO BUILD A SNOWMAN WITH ME?

Horn piece

White bricks for snow-capped mountain

MOUNTAIN

Build outward on the chest to make the yeti look chunkier

SPECIAL BRICK

This horn piece (also known as a large barb) makes a great yeti horn. You could use it for a beak or nose, too.

YETI

Icy-blue toes

SEARCH FOR BIGFOOT

The mysterious Bigfoot is thought to live deep in the woods. These hairy creatures are so hard to track down that some people don't believe they exist. It might be easier to build your own!

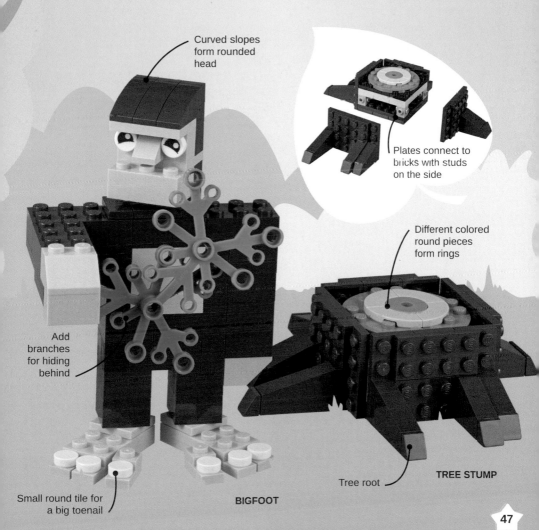

Curved slopes form rounded head

Plates connect to bricks with studs on the side

Different colored round pieces form rings

Add branches for hiding behind

Tree root

TREE STUMP

Small round tile for a big toenail

BIGFOOT

ONCE UPON A TIME

"There was a brave princess who yearned for an adventure ..." Tell a magical fairy tale with your LEGO® bricks. What will your imagination dream up?

I'M NOT SCARED OF YOU, GIGANTIC SPIDER!

LEGO® Technic angled connector

Move your minifigures across the different scenes

YOU LOOK LIKE YOU'VE SEEN A GHOST!

PART 1: THE FOREST OF FEAR

Hinge brick allows ghost to suddenly pop out!

ARRRGH!

Swap the minifigure's head for different facial expressions

Each scene is built on plates

PART 2: THE HAUNTED HILLS

*OH, **THIS** IS WHY IT'S CALLED THE STINKY SWAMP!*

Removing the minifigure's legs makes it look like she's wading

Swamp reed

1x1 round plate for green bubble

PART 3: THE STINKY SWAMP

TOP TIP
Keep your scenes simple and small. Focus on a few key moments in the story.

PHEW, MADE IT HOME IN TIME FOR DINNER!

Textured brick pattern

Four scenes tell the story of the princess's adventure

Clean skirt after the dunk in the swamp

PART 4: BACK AT THE PALACE

PUPPET SHOW

Build enchanting LEGO puppets and gather an audience for an unforgettable show. You control the puppets—and the magic! Why not make some wishes come true?

Slopes form pointy hat

Tiara

Mouth is a red plate

Sword for adventures

Wand

WIZARD

PRINCESS

Long LEGO Technic axle

TOP TIP

Your puppet will need a stick. Use a long, narrow plate or a LEGO Technic axle that fits into a 2x2 round brick with axle hole.

Tiny arm attaches to brick with stud on the side

Sturdy helmet

PALACE GUARD

Round plate for chest armor

Angle plates form base of crown

Witchy green skin tone

Gray bricks for beard

Plate with clip for holding broom

KING

WITCH

FAIRY-TALE CASTLES

You only need a handful of bricks to build magical mini LEGO castles with turrets and spires. Will you make yours look inviting or spooky?

SPECIAL BRICK

The 1x1 headlight brick has two studs and two holes that other bricks can connect to. The holes look like mini windows and doors, too!

THIS CASTLE IS A BIT SMALL FOR ME!

Turret with cone-shaped roof

Tiny window

Pathway to entrance

GRAND CASTLE

Corner panel piece for high wall

MICRO CASTLE

Turret

TINY CASTLE

4x4 base plate

Slope bricks top the turrets

Build turrets at different heights

Colorful cones for fall trees

FOREST CASTLE

Dome with spire

Grille piece

WELCOME TO MY MINI QUEENDOM

Arch brick creates majestic entrance

MYSTICAL CASTLE

ROARING DRAGONS

Some dragons are scary, but others are friendly and even bring good luck. What powers does your dragon have? You could add wings or fiery breath. Roooarrr!

⭐ SPECIAL BRICK

Attach wings with ball joints to make them flap up and down. You could use ball joints on tails to make them swish, too.

EEEK!

HMM ... I'D LIKE A KNIGHT-TIME SNACK!

Posable wings

Transparent red and yellow pieces attach to jumper plate

Stacked plates make little legs and feet

BABY DRAGON

SPLUTTER SPLUTTER! I'VE LOST MY PUFF!

Little yellow horns

Snout with teeth

CUTE DRAGON

Quarter-circle pieces for wings

Plates with clips attach to plate with bar

Wings attach with ball joints so they can be angled up and down

Long tail

Flame piece for fiery breath

FEARSOME DRAGON

Claws on wings

MISCHIEF MAKERS

These colorful pranksters love to get up to no good! Have you lost a particular LEGO brick? Is your sock drawer mysteriously empty? It may well be this troublesome trio!

Slope for ear

WHY DID THE BANANA GO TO THE DOCTOR?

Angle eyes for a mischievous look!

TRY THIS
Turn your mischievous models into bold fairies (known as sprites) by adding wings. Be warned: with wings, they might get up to even more mischief!

Plate with ring for hand

Head attaches
to jumper plate

Hands are
plates with
clips

Large, flappy
ears

Printed eye tile

*BECAUSE IT WAS
NOT PEELING
WELL!*

Upturned toes

CANDY
VILLAGE

Imagine living in a village that looks like your favorite foods! What will yours have? Fluffy marshmallow mountains? A birthday cake house? Lollipop trees? It all sounds good enough to eat!

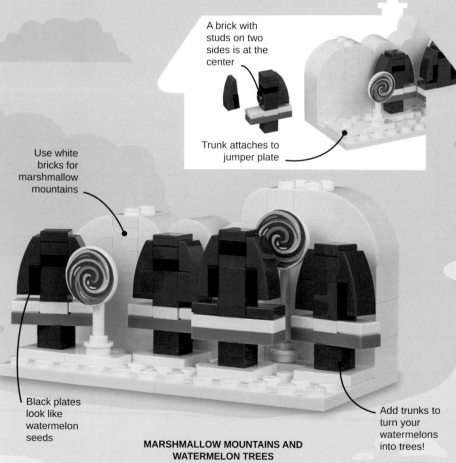

A brick with studs on two sides is at the center

Trunk attaches to jumper plate

Use white bricks for marshmallow mountains

Black plates look like watermelon seeds

Add trunks to turn your watermelons into trees!

MARSHMALLOW MOUNTAINS AND WATERMELON TREES

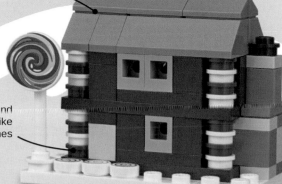

GINGERBREAD HOUSE

Purple icing roof

Stacked round plates look like candy canes

Don't forget to add a candle!

Colorful icing

Brown bricks look like chocolate cake

Jumper plates for door

BIRTHDAY CAKE HOUSE

THERE'S NO PLACE LIKE A TASTY HOME!

Cherry on top

Strawberry sauce made with pink plates

Tan bricks for ice-cream cone

ICE-CREAM CONE HOUSE

SUPER HEROES

These fantastic and fearless heroes use their magical powers to fight for good. Blue Bottle is super strong and The Green Fly can ... well, fly! What special powers will your super hero have?

Gigantic fists

GRRR! I AM THE STRONGEST!

Bulging muscle formed with curved slopes

Round tile for belt buckle

Long yellow boot

BLUE BOTTLE

TOP TIP

You can stand your super hero on top of a stack of transparent bricks to make it look like it is flying!

Side bun

ONLY IN SMELL, BLUE BOTTLE!

Outstretched arm for flying

THE GREEN FLY

1x1 plate with ring looks like a fist

Curved slope

Use bricks with side studs to attach arms and cape

Angled plate

Jumper plate and base plate for stability

61

EXTRAORDINARY ANIMALS

Sprinkle a little magic to make ordinary animals extraordinary! Change the colors or add wings, horns, and tails where they wouldn't usually be to make a unique fantasy creature.

★ TOP TIP

Plan your model before you begin building, so you can work out which recognizable animal parts you will include and how to attach them.

MEOW... ROAR!

Heart tile for cute kitten nose

Dragon wings attach with ball joints

Plates with clips for whiskers

Claw on wing

DRAGON-CAT

Plate attached to bricks with side studs

Slope for ear

Studs look like curly wool

Multicolored fleece

RAINBOW SHEEP

WANT A CARROT? NO PROB-LLAMA

Unicorn horn

Pink and purple shell

Sleepy eye

TORTI-CORN

Short tortoise legs

MARVELOUS VEHICLES

These elves get around in all kinds of magical ways! There's a spider walker that scuttles around on legs, a bike and a boat that can both also fly, and a submarine for underwater adventures.

Propeller

LET'S HEAD UP TO THE SKY!

Wings for adventures up high!

Boat piece

FLYING BOAT

Bar attaches to plate with clip

Wings slot onto LEGO® Technic axles

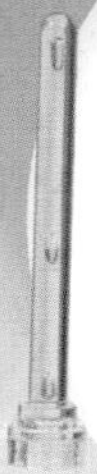

SPECIAL BRICK

Attach minifigures or small models to this transparent bar to make them look like they are flying! A clip or minifigure hand can grasp onto it.

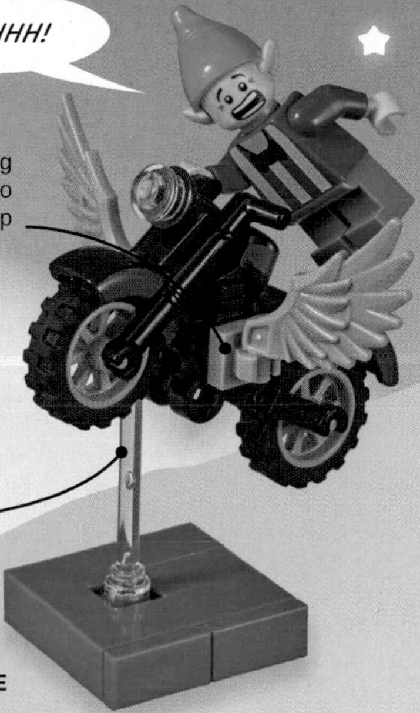
WAAAHHH!
Wing connects to plate with clip
Transparent bar

SKYBIKE

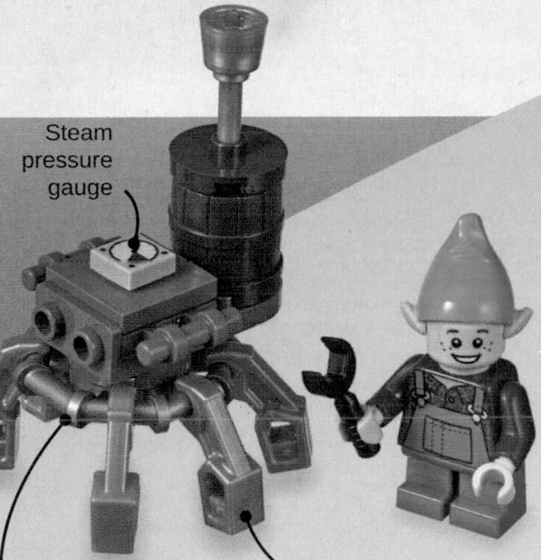
Steam pressure gauge
HOW MANY LEGS DOES A SPIDER HAVE AGAIN?
Plate with octagonal ring
Legs for scuttling

MECHANICAL STEAM SPIDER

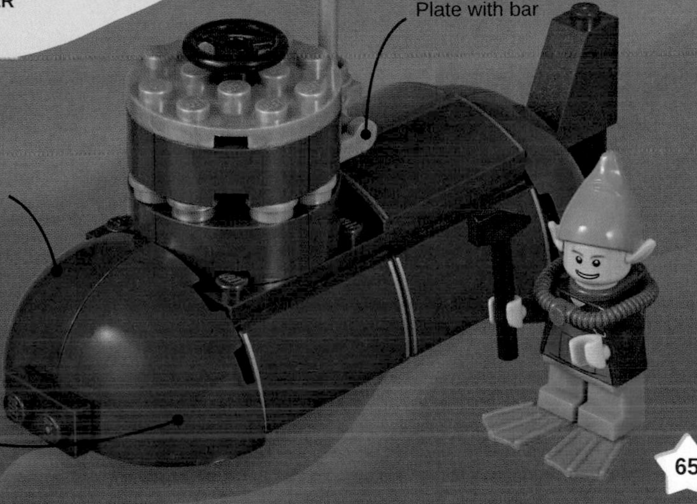
Periscope to see above water
Plate with bar
Quarter-dome piece
Streamlined hull

SUBMARINE

OVER THE
RAINBOW

When it is both sunny and rainy, a rainbow appears ... as if by magic! Will your LEGO® rainbow have a pot of gold at the end?

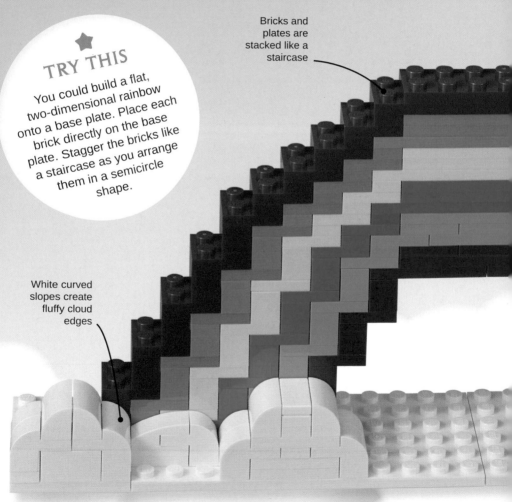

Bricks and plates are stacked like a staircase

TRY THIS

You could build a flat, two-dimensional rainbow onto a base plate. Place each brick directly on the base plate. Stagger the bricks like a staircase as you arrange them in a semicircle shape.

White curved slopes create fluffy cloud edges

RAINBOW

Two layers of small plates make up each layer of color

Angle the plates to make a quarter-circle shape

1x1 round bricks for gold coins

Pot handle is plate with bar

RAINBOW WITH POT OF GOLD

A POT OF GOLDEN HONEY? HOORAY!

White base plate blends in with clouds

GO STARGAZING

Can you spot a familiar shape in the stars of the night sky? These patterns of sparkling stars are called constellations. Map the magical night sky with your LEGO bricks.

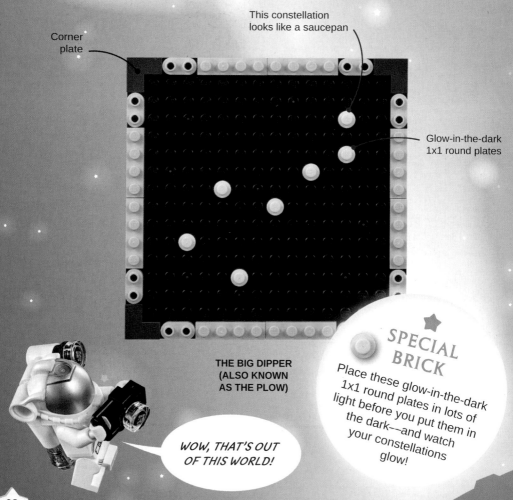

This constellation looks like a saucepan

Corner plate

Glow-in-the-dark 1x1 round plates

THE BIG DIPPER (ALSO KNOWN AS THE PLOW)

SPECIAL BRICK

Place these glow-in-the-dark 1x1 round plates in lots of light before you put them in the dark—and watch your constellations glow!

WOW, THAT'S OUT OF THIS WORLD!

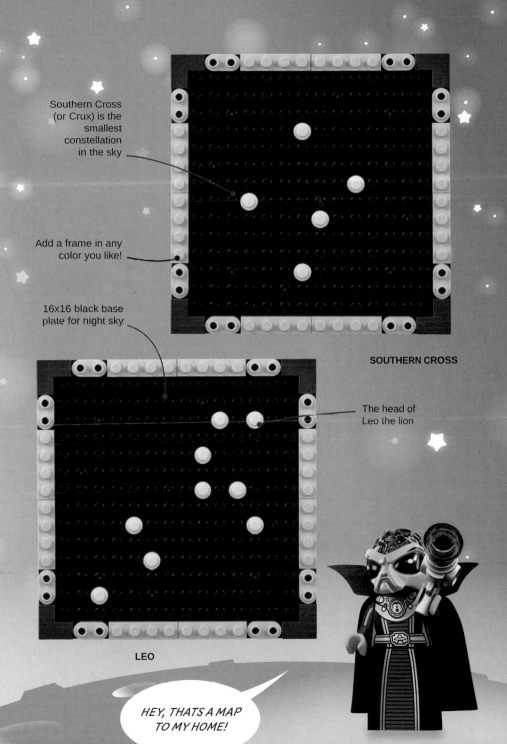

Southern Cross (or Crux) is the smallest constellation in the sky

Add a frame in any color you like!

16x16 black base plate for night sky

SOUTHERN CROSS

The head of Leo the lion

LEO

HEY, THATS A MAP TO MY HOME!

Senior Editor Helen Murray
Senior Designer Guy Harvey
Senior Production Editor Marc Staples
Senior Production Controller Louise Daly
Managing Editor Paula Regan
Managing Art Editor Jo Connor
Publishing Director Mark Searle
Model Photography Gary Ombler

Models designed and created by
Emily Corl, Rod Gillies, and Kevin Hall

Dorling Kindersley would like to thank: Randi
Sørensen, Heidi K. Jensen, Paul Hansford, Martin
Leighton Lindhardt, Nina Koopmann, Charlotte
Neidhardt, and Torben Vad Nissen at the LEGO
Group; Sam Bartlett for initial design work; Julia
March for proofreading, and Megan Douglass
for Americanizing.

First American Edition, 2021
Published in the United States by DK Publishing
1745 Broadway, 20th Floor, New York, New York
10019

Page design copyright ©2021 Dorling
Kindersley Limited
DK, a Division of Penguin Random House LLC
22 23 24 25 10 9 8 7 6 5 4 3
010–321738–Aug/2021

A catalog record for this book is available from the
Library of Congress.

ISBN 978-0-7440-2784-6

Printed and bound in China

For the curious

www.dk.com

www.LEGO.com

MEET THE BUILDERS

EMILY CORL

Emily is a professional
LEGO® brick artist and
builder. She loves the fairy
door model as she can
imagine knocking on the
door and a little fairy
opening it!

ROD GILLIES

Rod is a LEGO fan who
has always loved fantasy
and adventure stories,
and LEGO® Castle. His
favorite models to build
were the magical puppet
show characters.

KEVIN HALL

Kevin runs his own
company creating LEGO
models. He had great fun
designing different styles
of fairy-tale castles at a
micro scale. His top tip is
to never stop building!